Mary Lyn Ray

Welcome, Brown Bird

ILLUSTRATED BY Peter Sylvada

Harcourt, Inc.

Orlando Austin New York San Diego Toronto London

www.HarcourtBooks.com

Library of Congress Cataloging-in-Publication Data
Ray, Mary Lyn.
Welcome, Brown Bird/written by Mary Lyn Ray; illustrated by Peter Sylvada.
p. cm.
Summary: While a boy in North America urges his father not to cut down the trees where the wood thrush lives,
a boy in South America awaits the return of the bird that he calls "*la flauta*" for its flute-like song.
[1. Wood thrush—Fiction. 2. Birds—Migration—Fiction.]
I. Sylvada, Peter, ill. II. Title.
PZ7.R210154 We 2004
[E]—dc21 2002004056
ISBN 0-15-292863-4

First edition
G F E D C B A

Printed in Singapore

The illustrations in this book were done in oils.
The display type was hand-lettered by Georgia Deaver.
The text type was set in Humana Serif Light.
Color separations by Bright Arts Ltd., Hong Kong
Printed and bound by Tien Wah Press, Singapore
This book was printed on totally chlorine-free Stora Enso Matte paper.
Production supervision by Sandra Grebenar and Pascha Gerlinger
Designed by Judythe Sieck

For Jane, who also knew the thrush—M. L. R.

For my brother, Chris—P. S.

A boy lived at the edge of a hemlock woods.
In March he watched the snow melt.
In April he saw the grass grow green.
Then he began to listen.

Every day at dusk he listened.
And before April turned to May,
he heard what he waited for.

A song floated from deep in the dark hemlocks—
the thrush.
The boy honored it by listening.

When his father wanted to clear the trees to make a field for corn,
the boy said, "No, the thrush lives there."
His father remembered the bird who sang at the close of the day
and again at the coming of light.
And he let the trees stand.

So the thrush sang for the boy its silvery circular song.

Until one day the woods were quiet.
The light had changed. The air was no longer warm.

Summer had gone, and the thrush, too.

Deep in a damp forest, a mother called a boy to bed.

But the boy lingered and listened.

"*La flauta*," he told her, "*está aquí*."

There were brighter birds to look at, but none sang like the thrush.
All summer the boy had waited.
When heavy rains began in the fall, and vines and leaves dripped
in wet trees, he had known his bird would return soon.

Its song was the song of a clay flute.

When his father wanted to cut the trees to sell at the mill,
the boy said, "No, *la flauta vive acá.*"
His father remembered the bird who brought song.
And he let the trees stand.

So the thrush sang its song. And the boy listened.
Fall turned to winter, and winter turned to spring.

Then one day the thrush was not there.

Twenty-eight nights and twenty-eight days it flew north.

At the edge of a hemlock woods, a boy had been waiting while leaves
on the maples fell yellow and red, and snow made the hills white.
While snow melted and green grew back, he had waited.
Now he heard the thrush again.

Neither boy knew where the brown bird went.

Only the bird knew they were brothers.

A NOTE FROM THE AUTHOR

For all that even the closest watchers of birds have discovered about migration, still there is such mystery. How does the wood thrush that sings in the hemlocks beyond my barn in New Hampshire know to come *here*, to *this* farm, to *this* tree every year? How do the millions of other birds that migrate know their destination so exactly? How do they know the way? How do they know when to begin their flight so they arrive within a week of the same date they arrived the year before?

What we do know only enlarges the mystery. As winter becomes spring and summer becomes fall, changes in the amount of daylight trigger a hormonal change in migrating birds, and they begin to eat more to store energy for the long flight ahead. In flight they apparently use the stars, the moon and sun, the earth's magnetic field, and visible geography to help them find their way. But exactly how this happens, we don't know.

The thrush that summers in mixed pine and hardwoods across the eastern United States spends fall, winter, and early spring in tropical rain forests. Winter grounds range from eastern Mexico to Central America (primarily the Caribbean slope of Guatemala, Honduras, Nicaragua, and Costa Rica), Panama, and northwestern Colombia. There are thousands of miles between summer and winter. Actual flying time is thought to be twelve to fifteen days, but migration requires some twenty-eight days because flight is not continuous. Like other songbirds, the thrush flies at night, then rests and feeds during the day, sometimes staying for a day or two.

Many birds don't survive the trip. And now, increasingly, the birds that arrive find the habitat they depend on is gone. Every year more has been destroyed. Northern forests are being converted to lumber, house lots, building lots, and parking lots. Tropical forests are similarly being cleared for lumber and cropland or other commercial uses. Nesting sites are gone, shelter and food sources are gone, and predation by other birds and animals is more likely.

Of all songbirds, the thrush is one of those most threatened by loss of woodland. Every year there are fewer thrushes in summer and winter grounds. Every year there is less thrush song.

Each spring I wait for the return of the thrush. It used to be I'd begin listening in April for *when* it came back. Now, every year, it is *if*.

When I protected this old farm in New Hampshire as conservation land, I thought I was preserving land. Now I see I was also protecting song. But random protection isn't enough. At both ends of the migration route, in every place where we want to hear the thrush sing, we will have to find ways of integrating habitat for ourselves *and* this small brown bird, so there will always be song in the forest.

—M. L. R.